Happy Easter, Kevin—
from Grandma and
Grandpa Rogers— 1987

Editors: Ann Redpath, Etienne Delessert
Art Director: Rita Marshall
Publisher: George R. Peterson, Jr.

Copyright © 1983 Creative Education, Inc., 123 S. Broad Street,
Mankato, Minnesota 56001, USA. American Edition.
Copyright © 1983 Grasset & Fasquelle, Paris – Editions 24 Heures, Lausanne. French Edition.
International copyrights reserved in all countries.

Library of Congress Catalog Card No.: 83-71182
Grimm, Jakob and Wilhelm; Hansel and Gretel
Mankato, MN: Creative Education, Inc.; 32 pages. ISBN: 0-87191-935-4

Printed in Switzerland by Imprimeries Réunies S.A. Lausanne.

HANSEL & GRETTEL

JAKOB & WILHELM GRIMM
illustrated by
MONIQUE FELIX

CREATIVE EDUCATION INC.

ONCE UPON A TIME

THERE dwelt at the edge of a large forest a poor woodcutter with his wife and two children; the boy was called Hansel and the girl Grettel. He had little enough to live on, and once, when there was a great famine in the land, he couldn't even provide them with daily bread. One night, as he was tossing about in bed, full of cares and worry, he sighed and said to his wife:

"What's to become of us? How are we to support our poor children, now that we have nothing more for ourselves?"

"I'll tell you what, husband," answered the woman. "Early tomorrow morning we will take the children out into the thickest part of the wood. There we shall light a fire for them and give them each a piece of bread; then we'll go on to our work and leave them alone. They won't be able to find their way home, and we shall thus be rid of them."

"No, wife," said her husband, "that I won't do; how could I find it in my heart to leave my children alone in the wood? The wild beasts would soon come and tear them to pieces."

"Oh! You fool," said she, "then we must all four die of hunger, and you may just as well go and plane the boards for our coffins." And she left him no peace till he consented.

"But I can't help feeling sorry for the poor children," added the husband.

The children, too, had not been able to sleep for hunger, and had heard what their stepmother had said to their father. Grettel wept bitterly and spoke to Hansel. "Now it's all up with us."

"No, no, Grettel," said Hansel, "don't fret yourself; I'll find a way to escape, don't fear."

And when the old people had fallen asleep he got up, slipped on his little coat, opened the back door and stole out. The moon was shining clearly, and the white pebbles which lay in front of the house glittered like bits of silver. Hansel bent down and filled his pocket with as many of them as he could. Then he went back and said to Grettel:

"Be comforted, my dear little sister, and go to sleep. God will not desert us." And he lay down in bed again.

At daybreak, even before the sun was up, the woman came and woke the two children:

"Get up, you lazy-bones, we're all going to the forest to fetch wood."

She gave them each a bit of bread and spoke:

"There's something for your luncheon, but don't you eat it up before, for it's all you'll get."

Grettel took the bread under her apron, as Hansel had the stones in his pocket. Then they all set out together on the way to the forest.

After they had walked for a while, Hansel stood still and looked back at the house every so often. His father observed him, and asked:

"Hansel, what are you gazing at there, and why do you always remain behind? Take care, and don't lose your footing."

"Oh! father," said Hansel, "I am looking back at my white kitten, which is sitting on the roof, waving me a farewell."

The woman exclaimed:

"What a donkey you are! That isn't your kitten, that's the morning sun shining on the chimney."

But Hansel had not looked back at his kitten, but had always dropped one of the white pebbles out of his pocket onto the path.

When they had reached the middle of the forest, the father said:

"Now, children, go and fetch a lot of wood, and I'll light a fire so you won't feel cold."

Hansel and Grettel heaped up brushwood till they had made a pile nearly the size of a small hill. The brushwood was set afire, and when the flames leaped high the woman said:

"Now lie down at the fire, children, and rest yourselves. We are going into the forest to cut down wood. When we've finished we'll come back and fetch you."

Hansel and Grettel sat down beside the fire, and at midday ate their little bits of bread. They heard the strokes of the axe, so they thought their father was quite near. But it was no axe they heard, just a bough he had tied on to a dead tree that was blown about by the wind. And when they had sat for a long time, their eyes closed with fatigue. They fell fast asleep.

When they awoke at last, it was pitch-dark. Grettel began to cry, and said:

"How are we ever to get out of the wood?"

But Hansel comforted her.

"Wait a bit," he said, "till the moon is up, and then we'll find our way sure enough."

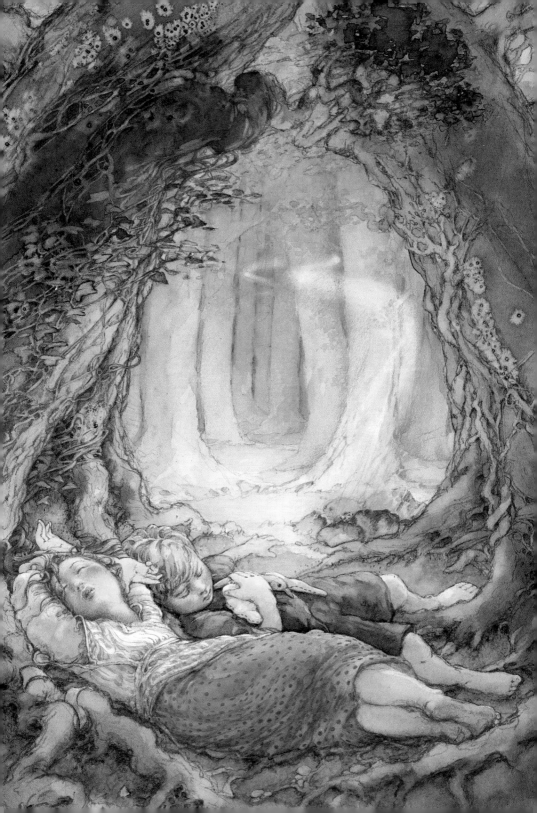

And when the full moon had
risen, he took his sister by the
hand and followed the pebbles,
which shone like new three-
penny bits, and showed them
the path. They walked all
through the night, and at daybreak reached their father's
house again. They knocked at
the door, and when the woman
opened it she exclaimed:

"You naughty children, what
a time you've slept in the wood!
We thought you were never
going to come back."

But the father rejoiced, for
he had felt guilty for leaving
his children behind by themselves.

Not long afterwards there was again great famine in the land, and the children heard their mother address their father in bed one night:

"Everything is eaten up once more; we have only half a loaf in the house, and when that's done it's all up with us. The children must be gotten rid of. We'll lead them deeper into the wood this time, so that they won't be able to find their way out again. There is no other way of saving ourselves."

The man's heart smote him heavily, and he thought:

"Surely it would be better to share the last bite with one's children!"

But his wife wouldn't listen to his arguments, and did nothing but scold him. If a man yields once, he's done for. And because he had given in the first time, he was forced to do so the second.

But the children were awake, and had heard the conversation. When the old people were asleep Hansel got up, and wanted to go out and pick up pebbles again, as he had done the first time; but the woman had barred the door, and Hansel couldn't get out. But he consoled his little sister, and said:

"Don't cry, Grettel, and sleep peacefully, for God is sure to help us."

At early dawn the woman came and made the children get up. They received their bit of bread, but it was even smaller than the time before. On the way to the wood Hansel crumbled it in his pocket, and every few minutes he stood still and dropped a crumb on the ground.

"Hansel, what are you stopping and looking about you for?" asked the father.

"I'm looking back at my little pigeon, which is sitting on the

roof waving me a farewell," answered Hansel.

"Fool!" said the wife, "that isn't your pigeon, it's the morning sun glittering on the chimney."

But Hansel gradually threw all his crumbs on to the path. The woman led the children still deeper into the forest, farther than they had ever been in their lives. Then a big fire was lit again, and the mother said:

"Just sit down there, children, and if you're tired you can sleep a bit; we're going into the forest to cut down wood, and in the evening when we're finished, we'll come back to fetch you."

At midday Grettel divided her bread with Hansel, for he had dropped his all along their path. Then they fell asleep, and evening passed away, but no-body came to the poor children.

They didn't awake till it was pitch-dark, and Hansel comforted his sister, saying:

"Only wait, Grettel, till the moon rises, then we shall see the bread-crumbs I scattered along the path; they will show us the way back to the house."

When the moon appeared they got up, but they found no crumbs, for the thousands of birds that fly about the woods and fields had picked them all up.

"Never mind," said Hansel to Grettel. "You'll see we'll still find a way out." But all the same they did not.

They wandered about the whole night, and the next day, from morning till evening, but they could not find a path out of the wood. They were very hungry, too, for they had nothing to eat but a few berries they found growing on the ground. And at last were so tired that their legs refused to carry them any longer, so they lay down under a tree and fell fast asleep.

On the third morning after they had left their father's house, they set about their wandering again, but only got deeper and deeper into the wood. Now they felt that if help did not come to them soon, they must perish. At midday they saw a beautiful little snow-white bird sitting on a branch. It sang so sweetly that they stopped and listened to it. And when its song was finished it flapped its wings and flew on in front of them. They followed it and came to a little house, where the bird perched on the roof.

And when they came quite near they saw that the cottage was made of bread and roofed with cakes, while the window was made of transparent sugar.

"Now," said Hansel, "we'll have a feast. I'll eat a bit of the roof, and you, Grettel, can eat some of the window, which you'll find a sweet morsel."

Hansel stretched up his hand and broke off a little bit of the roof to see what it was like, and Grettel went to the casement and began to nibble at it. Immediately a shrill voice called out from the room inside:

"Nibble, nibble, little mouse,
Who's nibbling my house?"

The children answered:

"Tis Heaven's own child,
The tempest wild,"

and went on eating, without putting themselves about. Hansel, who thoroughly appreciated the roof, tore down a big bit of it, while Grettel pushed out a whole round window-pane, and sat down to enjoy it.

Suddenly the door opened, and an ancient dame leaning on a staff hobbled out. Hansel and Grettel were so terrified that they let what they had in their hands fall. But the old woman shook her head and said:

"Oh, ho! you dear children. Who led you here? Just come in and stay with me; no ill shall befall you."

She took them both by the hand and led them into the house, and laid a most sumptuous dinner before them—milk and sugared pancakes, with apples and nuts. After they had finished, two beautiful little white beds were prepared for them. When Hansel and Grettel lay down in them they felt as if they had gone to heaven.

The woman had appeared to be most friendly, but she was really an old witch who had waylaid the children, and had only built the little bread house in order to lure them in. When anyone came into her power she killed, cooked, and ate him, and held a regular feast-day for the occasion. Now witches have red eyes, and cannot see far, but, like beasts, they have a keen sense of smell, and know when human beings pass by. When Hansel and Grettel fell into her hands she laughed maliciously, and said jeeringly:

"I've got them now; they shan't escape me."

Early in the morning, before the children were awake, she rose up. And when she saw them both sleeping so peacefully, with their round rosy cheeks, she muttered to herself:

"That'll be a dainty bite."

Then she seized Hansel with her bony hand and carried him into a little stable, and barred the door on him. He might scream as much as he liked, it did him no good. Then she went to Grettel, shook her till she awoke, and cried:

"Get up, you lazy-bones, fetch water and cook something for your brother. When he's fat I'll eat him up."

Grettel began to cry bitterly, but it was of no use; she had to do what the wicked witch bade her.

So the best food was cooked for poor Hansel, but Grettel got nothing but crab-shells. Every morning the old woman hobbled out to the stable and cried:

"Hansel, put out your finger, that I may feel if you are getting fat."

But Hansel always stretched out a bone, and the old dame, whose eyes were dim, couldn't see it, and thinking it was Hansel's finger, wondered why he fattened so slowly. When four weeks passed and Hansel still remained thin, she lost patience and determined to wait no longer.

"Hi! Grettel," she called to the girl, "be quick and get some water. Hansel may be fat or thin, but I'm going to kill him tomorrow and cook him."

Oh! how the poor little sister sobbed as she carried the water, and how the tears rolled down her cheeks!

"Kind heaven help us now!" she cried; "if only the wild beasts in the wood had eaten us, then at least we should have died together."

"Just hold your peace," said the old hag. "It won't help you."

Early in the morning Grettel had to go out and hang up the kettle full of water, and light the fire.

"First we'll bake," said the old dame. "I've already heated the oven and kneaded the dough."

She pushed Grettel out to the oven, from which fiery flames were already appearing.

"Creep in," said the witch, "and see if it's properly heated, so that we can shove in the bread."

For when she had gotten Grettel in, she meant to close the oven and let the girl bake, that she might eat her up too. But Grettel perceived her intention, and spoke:

"I don't know how I'm to do it; how do I get in?"

"You silly goose!" said the hag, "the opening is big enough. See, I could get in myself." And she crawled towards it, and poked her head into the oven.

Then Grettel gave her a shove that sent her right in, shut the iron door, and drew the bolt. Gracious! How she yelled! It was quite horrible. But Grettel fled, and the wretched old woman was left to perish miserably.

Then Grettel flew straight to
Hansel, opened the little stable-
door, and cried:

"Hansel, we are free; the old
witch is dead."

Then Hansel sprang like a bird
out of a cage when the door is
opened. How they rejoiced,
and hugged each other, and
jumped for joy, and kissed one
another! And as they had no
longer any cause for fear, they
went into the old hag's house,
and there they found, in every
corner of the room, boxes with
pearls and precious stones.

"These are even better than
pebbles," said Hansel, and
filled his pockets full of them;
and Grettel said:

"I too will bring something
home." And she filled her
apron full.

"But now," said Hansel, "let's
go and get well away from the
witch's wood."

When they had wandered about for some hours they came to a big lake.

"We can't get over it," said Hansel. "I see no bridge of any sort or kind."

"Yes, and there's no ferry-boat either," answered Grettel. "But look, there swims a white duck; if I ask her she'll help us over." And she called out:

> *"Here are two children,*
> *Mournful very,*
> *Seeing neither*
> *Bridge nor ferry;*
> *Take us upon*
> *Your white back,*
> *And row us over,*
> *Quack, quack!"*

The duck swam towards them, and Hansel got on her back and asked his little sister to sit beside him.

"No," answered Grettel, "we should be too heavy a load for the duck; she shall carry us across separately."

The good bird did this, and when they were landed safely on the other side, and had gone on for a while, the wood became more and more familiar to them, and after a while they saw their father's house in the distance.

Then they began to run, and bounding into the room, they hugged their father. The man had not passed a happy hour since he left them in the wood, but the woman had died. Grettel shook out her apron so that the pearls and precious stones rolled about the room, and Hansel threw down one handful after the other out of his pocket. Thus all their troubles were ended, and they all lived happily ever afterwards.

My story is done. See! There runs a little mouse. Anyone who catches it may make himself a large fur cap out of it.